All for Me
and
None for All

For Kate, Andrew, and River—all for you!
–H.L.

For Graydon and Griffin.
–L.M.

Text copyright © 2012 by Helen Lester
Illustrations copyright © 2012 by Lynn Munsinger

Houghton Mifflin Books for Children is an imprint of Houghton Mifflin Harcourt Publishing Company.

www.hmhbooks.com

The text of this book is set in Garamond.
The illustrations are watercolor, pencil, and pen and ink.

Library of Congress Cataloging-in-Publication Data
is on file.
ISBN 978-0-547-68834-3

Manufactured in Mexico
RDT 10 9 8 7 6 5 4 3 2
4500357906

All for Me
and
None for All

Written by Helen Lester
Illustrated by Lynn Munsinger

Houghton Mifflin Books for Children
Houghton Mifflin Harcourt
BOSTON NEW YORK

Gruntly was a ball hog.
Not only did he refuse to share *his* toys with Hampshire and Berkshire,
but he helped himself to *theirs*.

Gruntly grabbed Yorky's shoes even though he already had far more shoes than feet.

And it got worse. Gruntly constantly snuck up on Woolworth and Cluck
to gather more fluff and feathers so *he* would have the poofiest pillows.
If there was a something, he wanted it all. All for himself.

"What a **HOG!**" snorted Hampshire, Berkshire, and Yorky.

"He bestows new meaning upon the word," wise Woolworth said wisely.

"Cluck," Cluck said, and nodded. She was a chicken of few words.

Clearly, Gruntly's companions were fed up with his greediness.

One day as Gruntly was skipping along, wolfing someone else's doughnut and collecting illegal flowers, he came upon a sign:

PLEASE DO NOT PICK THE FLOWERS

THE PARKS DEPARTMENT INVITES YOU TO A TREASURE HUNT ON SATURDAY.

"Oh yes!" exclaimed Gruntly. "A treasure! All for me!
Gold up to my belly,
silver to my snout,
Diamonds to my pointy ears—
that's what it's all about. Hey!"

When Saturday came, Gruntly was ready for action. The park ranger explained the rules of the treasure hunt to the eager hunters. "You will have three clues," she said. "I'll give you the first clue. If you follow that and the other clues, you'll find a treasure."

"Ooooooo," said Hampshire, Berkshire, and Yorky.
"A stupendously superb opportunity," observed wise
Woolworth.
"Cluck," agreed Cluck.
And over at the starting line, "Yes," hissed Gruntly.
"I'm going to be number one and get all the treasure.
All for me and none for all!"

The park ranger called out the first clue.

CLUE #1

"Go fifty steps
Then you will see
Clue number two
Under the—"

"SEA! Yes!"

Gruntly was in such a hurry to be in the lead, he didn't bother to hear the end of the clue. As the others headed off to look under the tree, Gruntly was racing toward the sea.

Gruntly did not get far. Gruntly got wet. So he slogged back. As he passed the tree, the second clue, which the other hunters had left behind, blew right into his hand.

CLUE #2

*To find the next clue
And make your heart sing
Go to the playground,
Look under the—*

Again Greedy Gruntly was so eager to be number one, he skipped the last word.

"I've got it!" he snorted. "WING! Look under the wing!"

Several annoyed and squawking birds later, Gruntly gave up the wing idea, and as he hurried past the playground swing he tripped over the last clue, which his companions had tossed in the grass.

CLUE #3

To find your own treasure
Turn left at the frog
And there it will be
Under a—

"I know! I know! I know!" cried Gruntly. "Under a HOG!
And there it will be, under a hog! Yes!"

Gruntly galloped on,
zoomed left at the frog,
and screeched to a halt.
He was surprised to find
his companions already
sitting on a log.

But no time to wonder. It was time for some serious hog-tipping.

"Pardon me. Move it, please. Sorry, Woolworth, didn't mean you. *Scusi.*"

When both the hogs had been tipped, with absolutely no treasure beneath them, Gruntly paused. And blinked. How could this be?

No gold. No silver. No diamonds.

"Wait a minute." Gruntly eyed the little bags the others were clutching. "Whatchagot?"

The little group backed away. "Trail mix," they answered, "our treasures."

"That's it? Trail mix? Seriously?" Gruntly was almost speechless as his mind tried to replace gold, silver, and diamonds with trail mix. This was stressful, but he did it. After all, trail mix was rather yummy. And crunchy. And sweet. And delicious.

"I don't suppose there might be some left for *ME?* All for *ME?*"
Gruntly's fellow hunters, fearing that he might grab at any moment,
gripped their little bags so tightly, they crackled.
Then Cluck, the chicken of few words, strutted forward.
She looked Gruntly in the eye and said, "Cluck."

"Look?" wondered
Gruntly. "Look where?"

Cluck pointed her ruffled wing toward the log. "Cluck."

"*There?*" asked Gruntly.

And then Cluck got down on her knees (or whatever chickens get down on) and pointed way low with her beak. "Cluck-cluck-cluck-cluck."

Cluck-cluck-cluck-cluck. Un-der-the-log.

Ohhhhh, now Gruntly got it.
Without even waiting as Cluck clucked *You-betcha* ("Cluck-cluckcluck"),
Gruntly looked under the log and grabbed his treasure.

His very own treasured treasure.

He was about to dig in . . .
But wait.

The others had saved it.
No one had touched it.
Or taken it.
Or snatched it.
Or grabbed it.
Or tried a nibble.
Or a gobble.
Or HOGGED it.

Gruntly was so moved by his companions' kindness
and honesty, there was only one thing to do.
Should he? *Would* he? *Could* he?
"*Cluck* cluck?" wondered Cluck.
As Gruntly moved closer, Hampshire, Berkshire,
and Yorky hugged their treasures, trembling.

Cluck continued to wonder.

And Woolworth pulled the wool over his eyes.

Gruntly looked at his worried companions.

"All . . ."

The little group took a deep breath. Gruntly just smiled.
"*Allllllll*most all for me. But some for all!"

Gruntly shared.